As Quiet As A

MOUSE

en Owen

illustrated by

Evgenia Golubeva

Edgar loved his
new baby sister.

Mabel was small and cute and
liked sleeping. But Edgar was
so noisy he kept waking her up.

"Edgar! You sound like a whole herd of elephants, not just one little one!" said Mum.

"Sorry," said Edgar.

"Wahhhh!"

Edgar tried his best to be quiet.

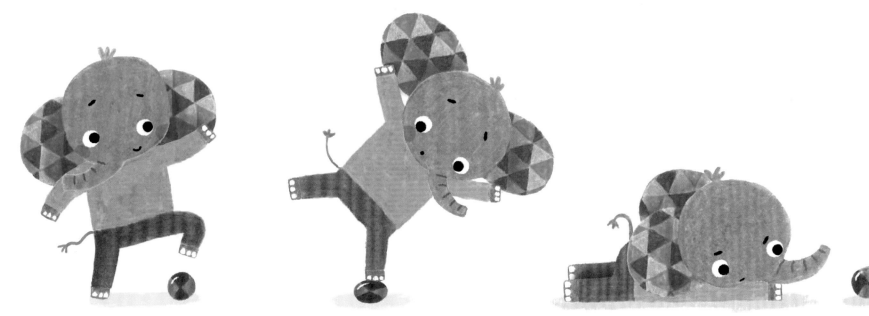

He tiptoed.

He crawled.

He even tried foot muffs.

"Edgar!" said Mum.

"You need to be as quiet as a mouse!"

"Why are you looking so sad?"
asked Edgar's friend, Ruby.

He told her about his noisy problem.
"I've got an idea!" she said.

So Edgar followed Ruby...

THUMP

THUMP

THUMP

All the way to Mouse School.

"Walk across the stage,"
said Mr Cheddar.

Mr Cheddar tapped his stick on the ground. "Goodness me! Not like that! Like this!" he said.

Edgar couldn't hear them at all! He sighed. "I'll never be that quiet," he thought.

Finally, it was time to take the Quiet Mouse Test.

Edgar and his friends walked and tiptoed and danced.

The audience clapped quietly.

Mr Cheddar beamed. "I am pleased to announce that Edgar has just become the first elephant ever to be officially as quiet as a mouse," he said.

Edgar was so proud he swished his trunk... very quietly, of course.

"Well done to all of our quiet winners...Now it's party time!"

as Quiet as a mouse

"Hurray!"

The mice cheered and rushed to the tables full of party food.

"Shhhh!" whispered Edgar's mum.
But she was too late...
"Wahhhh!" cried Mabel.

Mum covered up her ears.
"You sound like..."

The End

As Quiet As A Mouse

An original concept by author Karen Owen

© Karen Owen

Illustrations by Evgenia Golubeva

Published by MAVERICK ARTS PUBLISHING LTD

Studio 3A, City Business Centre, 6 Brighton Road,

Horsham, West Sussex, RH13 5BB

© Maverick Arts Publishing Limited September 2015 +44 (0)1403 256941

A CIP catalogue record for this book is available at the British Library.

ISBN 978-1-84886-172-5

Maverick
arts publishing
www.maverickbooks.co.uk